To Morgan for supporting.
To Erin for pushing.
To Bethany for creating.
To Leo for being.

Published by Peter Pauper Press, Inc.
202 Mamaroneck Avenue
White Plains, New York 10601 USA

Library of Congress Control Number: 2020934674

ISBN 978-1-4413-3506-7

Manufactured for Peter Pauper Press, Inc.
Printed in Hong Kong

7 6 5 4 3 2 1

Visit us at www.peterpauper.com

THE
STARING
CONTEST

NICHOLAS SOLIS

 Peter Pauper Press, Inc.
WHITE PLAINS, NEW YORK

Staring contest!

GO!

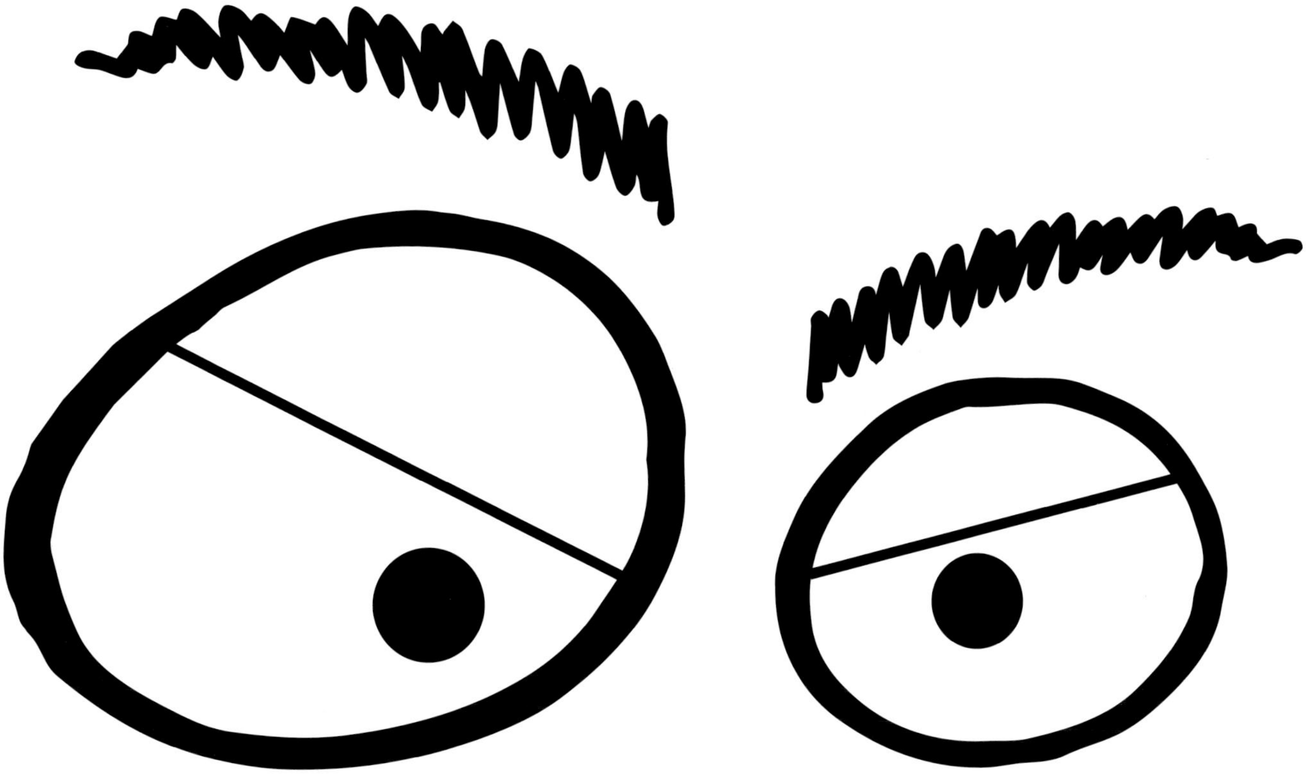

Ha, ha! I knew you weren't ready.

I'm totally going to win!

I can't believe you agreed to compete in a

staring contest with **ME**!

I'm a staring master!

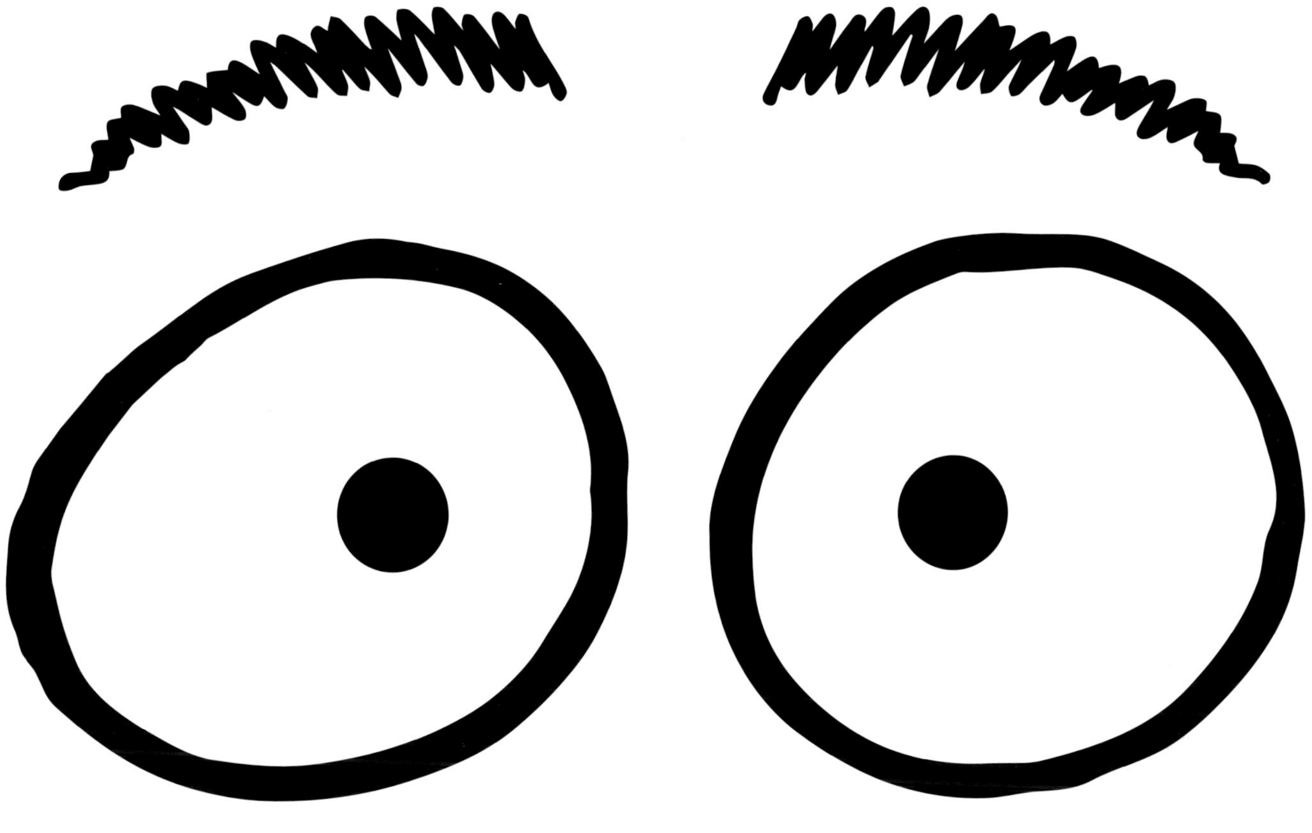

I can stare . . .

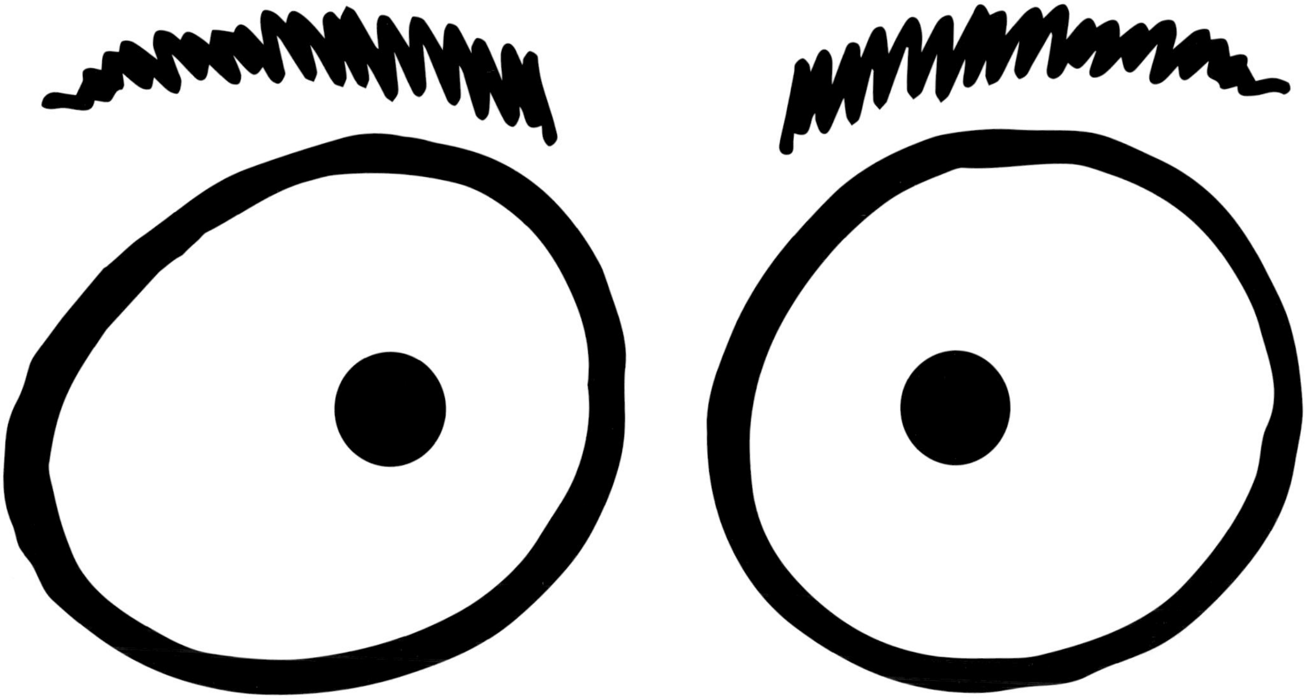

all . . .

day . . .

LONG!

And I'll never blink.

Not even if you blow in my eyes.

Go ahead. Try it.

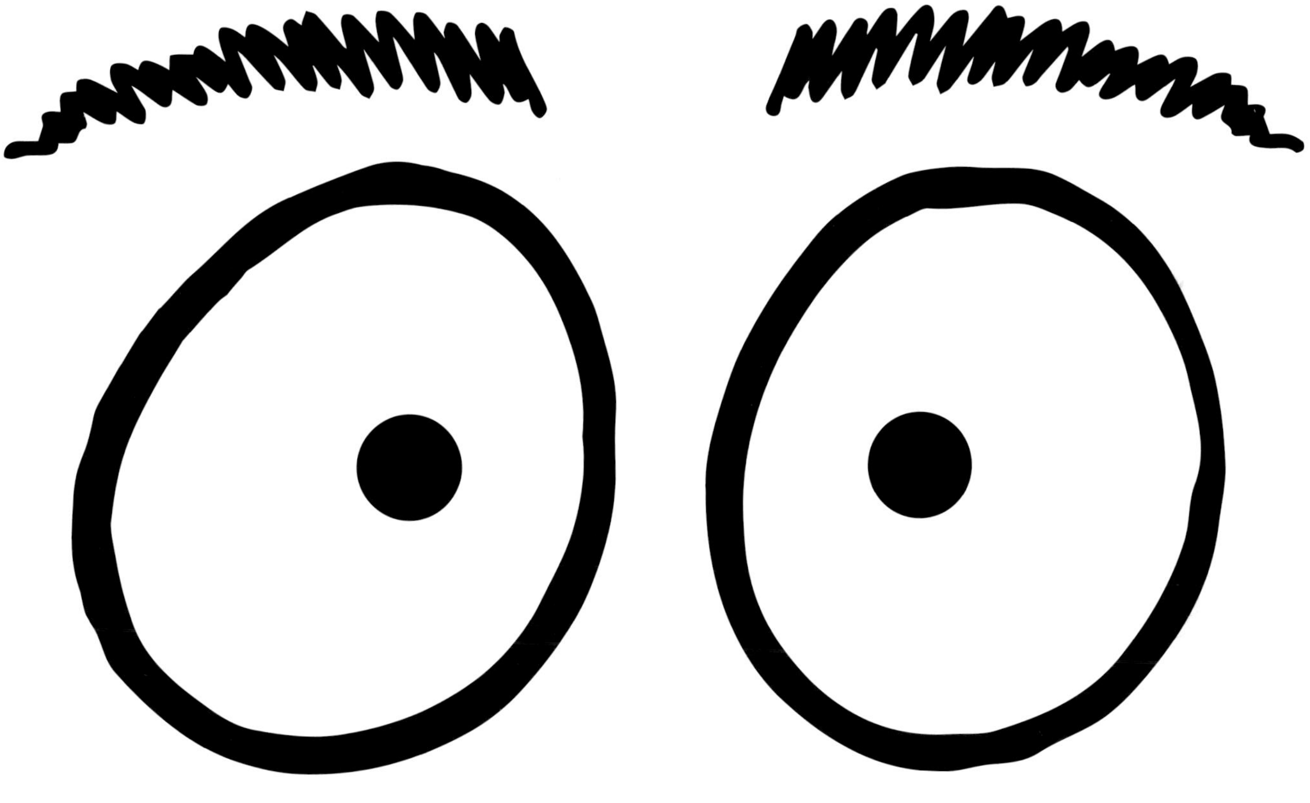

WHOA!

I can't believe you blew in my eyes.

That's cheating!

But I didn't blink.

Told you I'm the best.

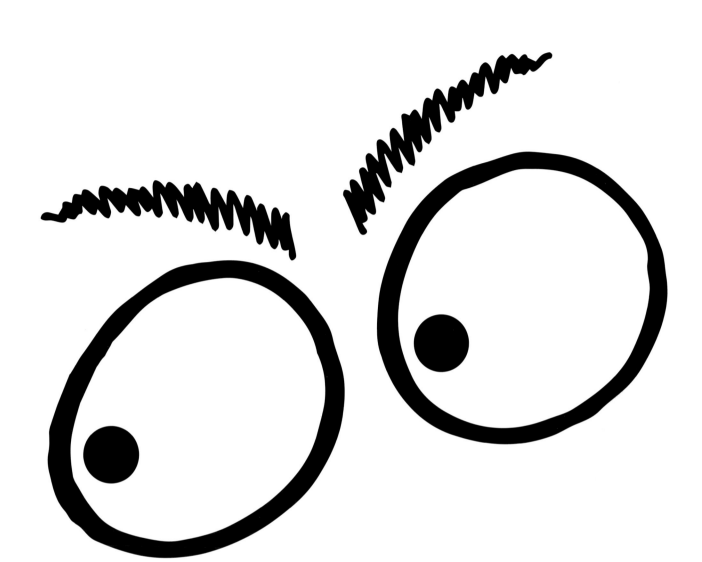

You probably think you're pretty good.

Let's see if you can keep your eyes on me . . .

when I go . . .

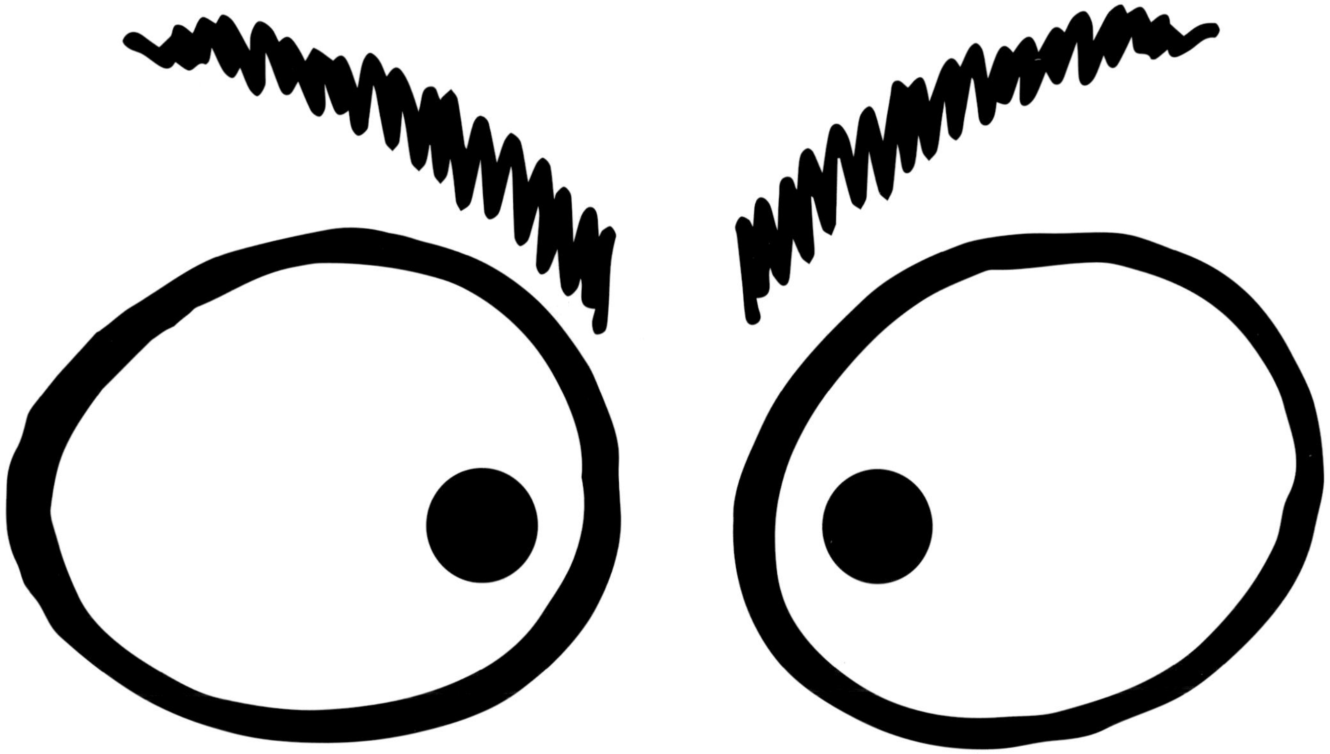

UP!

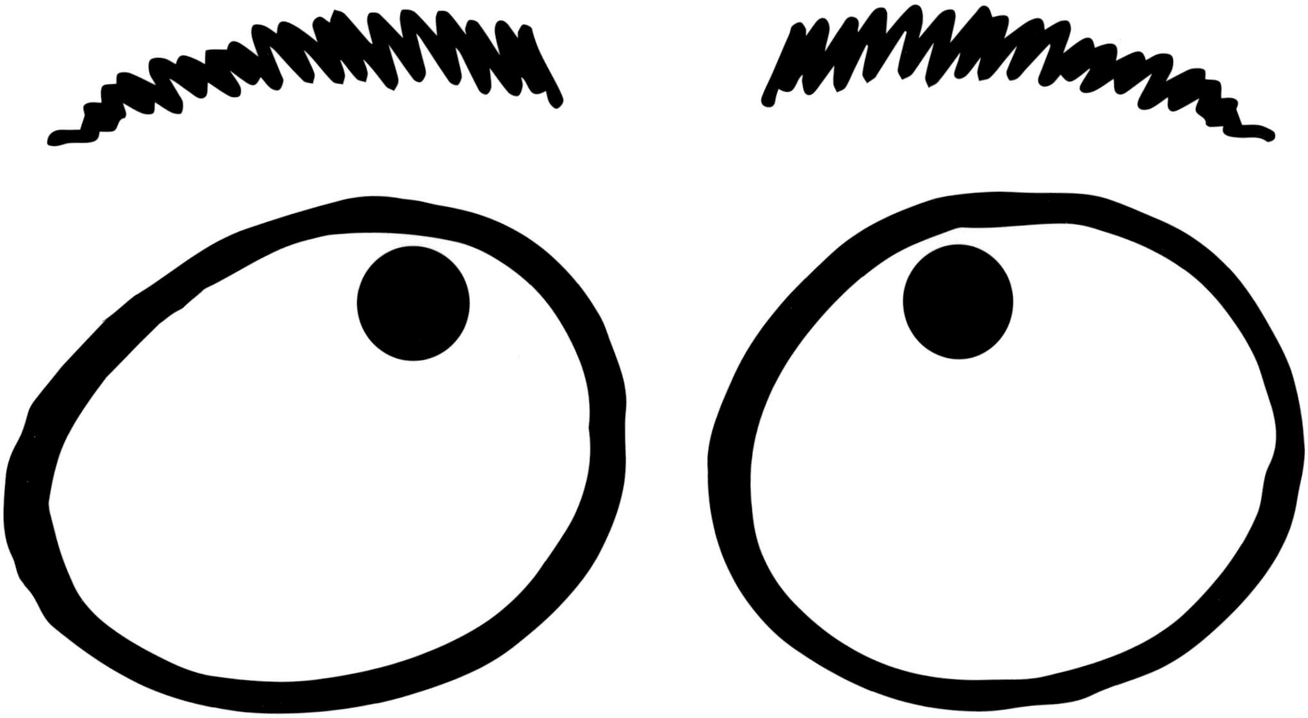

DOWN!

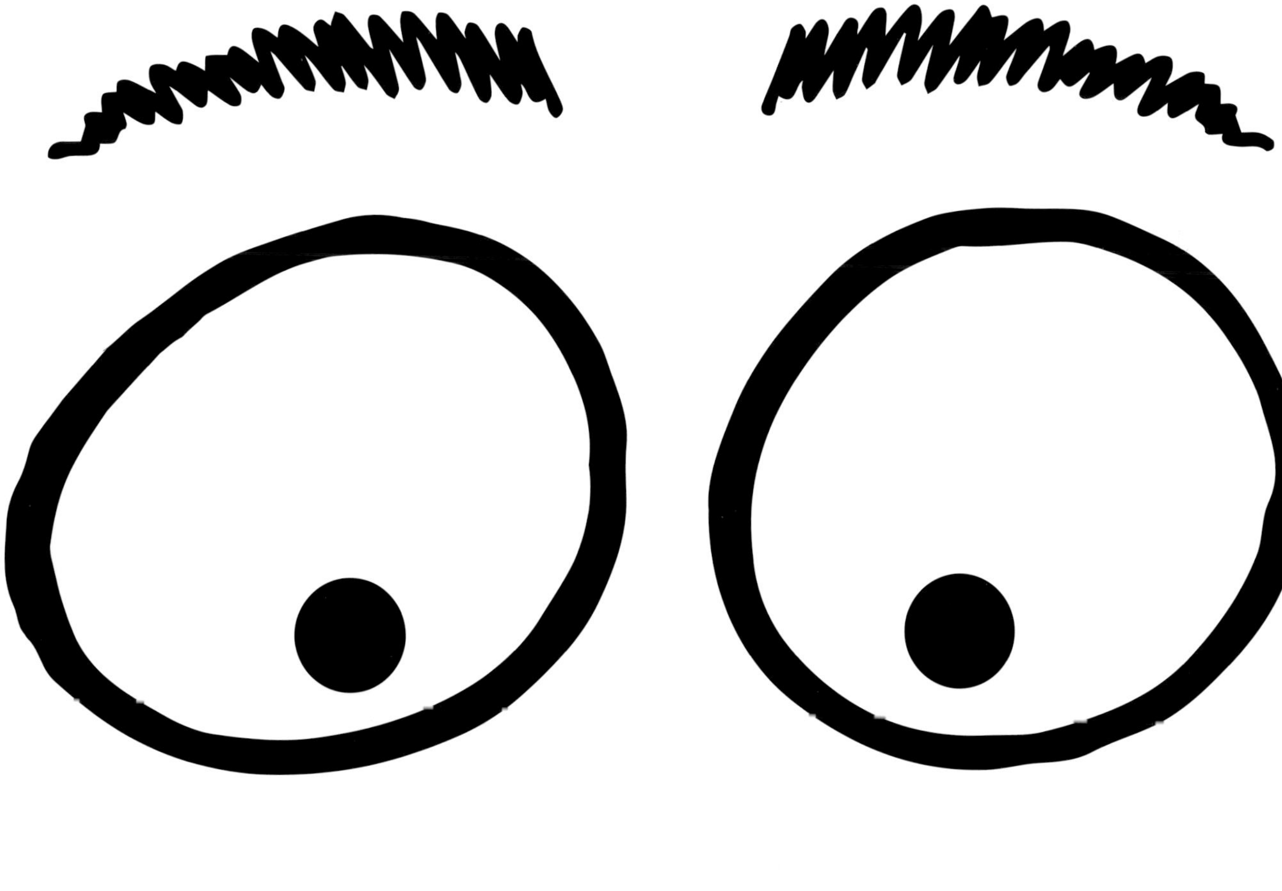

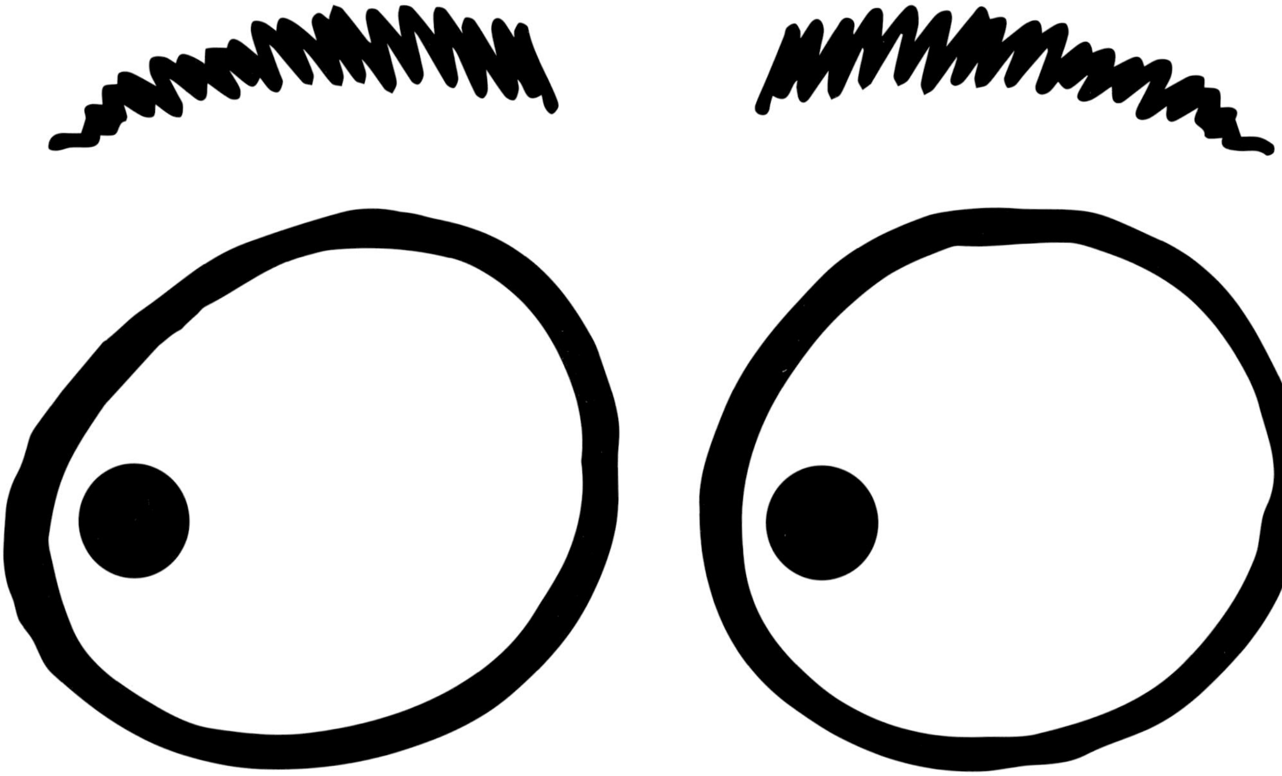

LEFT!

RIGHT!

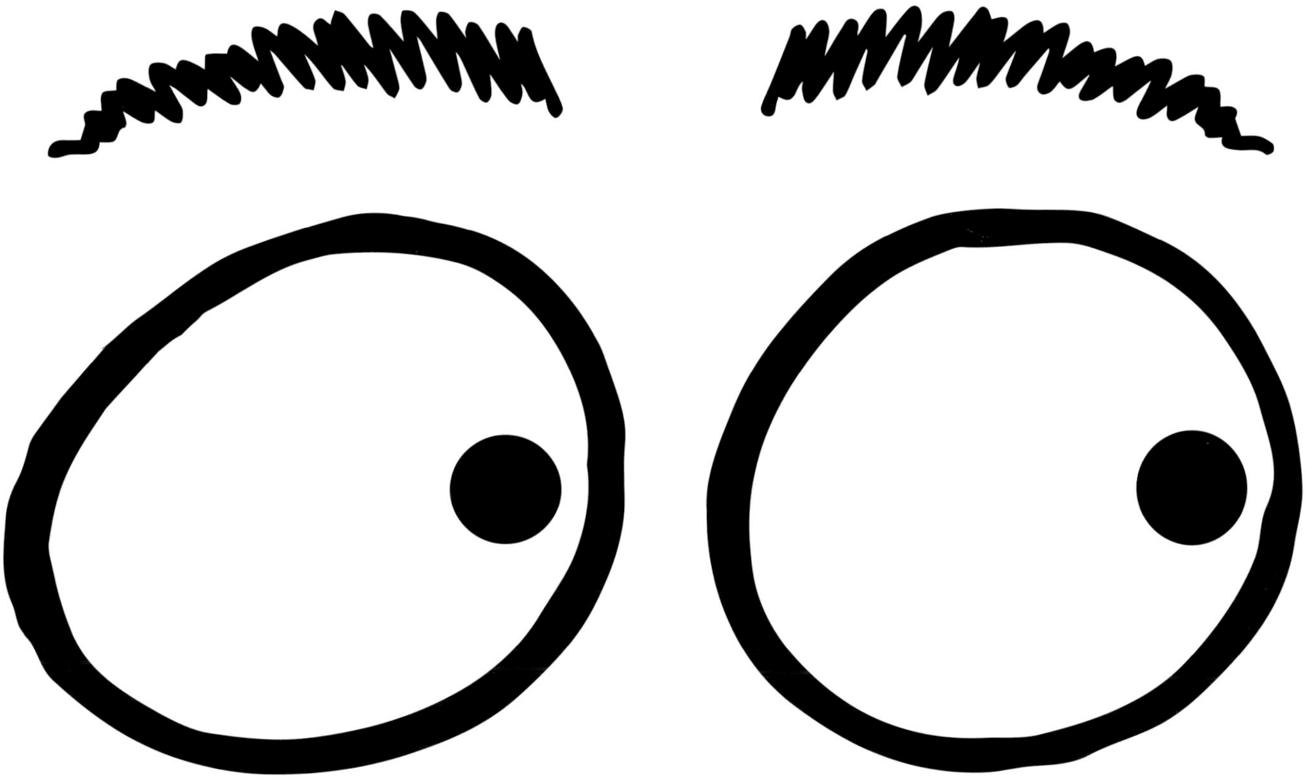

CRISS-CROSS!

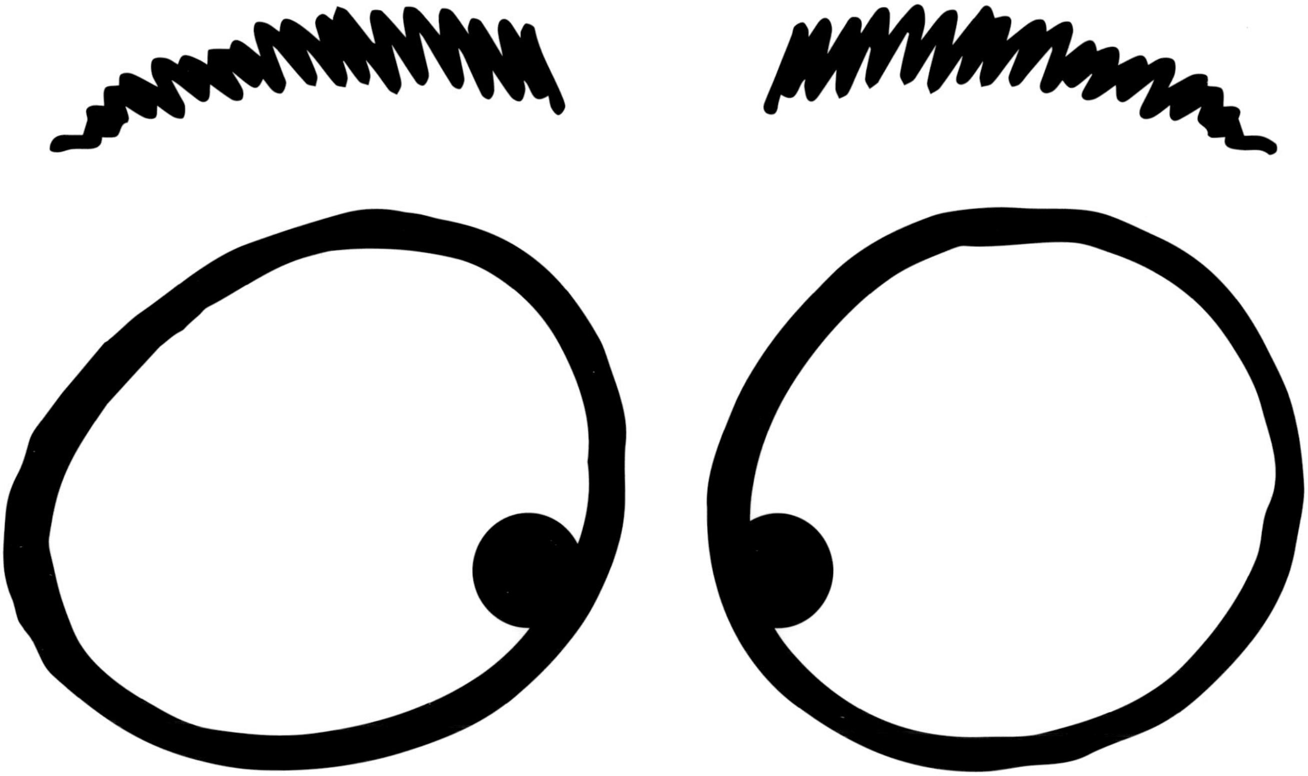

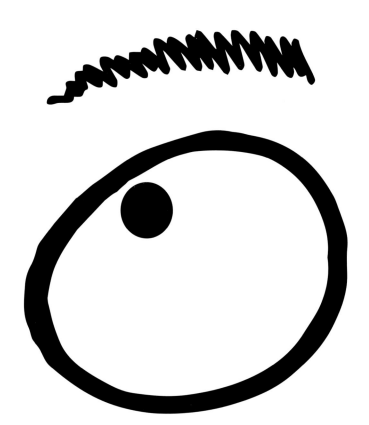

D I A G

ONAL!

Ok, ok.

You've got some skills.

The important thing to remember is that we

play

nice

and

FAIR.

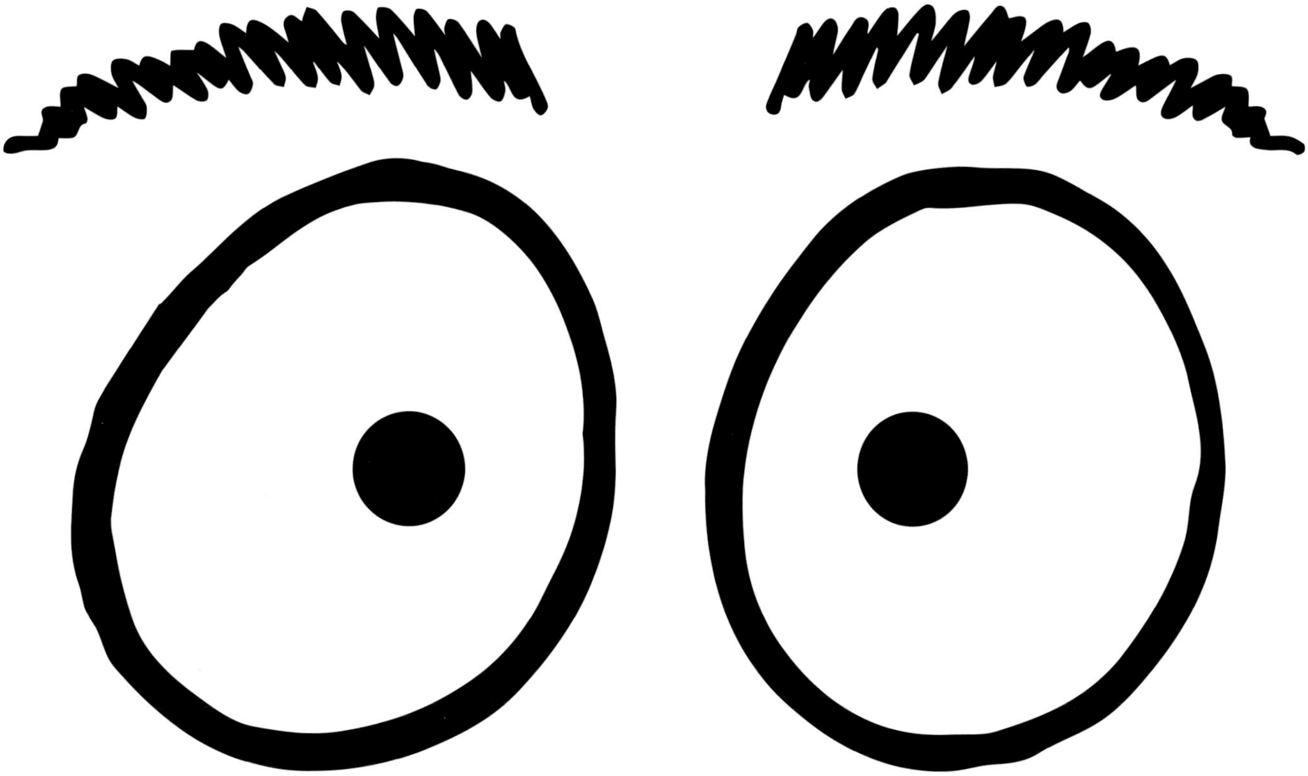

Oh no!

What's that behind you?

ALIENS have landed!

Your friend is sticking her tongue out at you!

LOOK!

WHOA! Check out that dancing monkey!

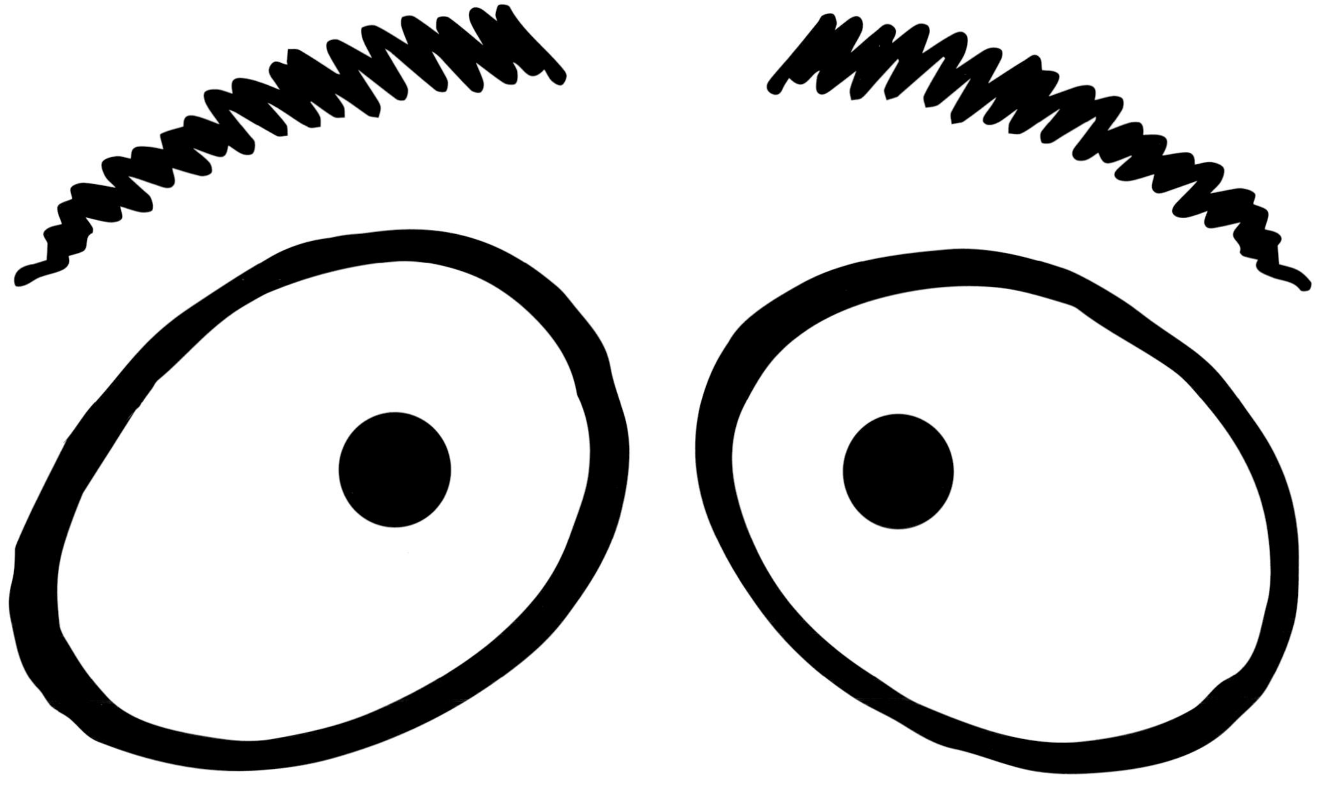

Hmmmmm. Still here, huh?

I thought you'd fall for that.

You're pretty good.

But you'll never beat me.

I'm a **CHAMPION** starer.

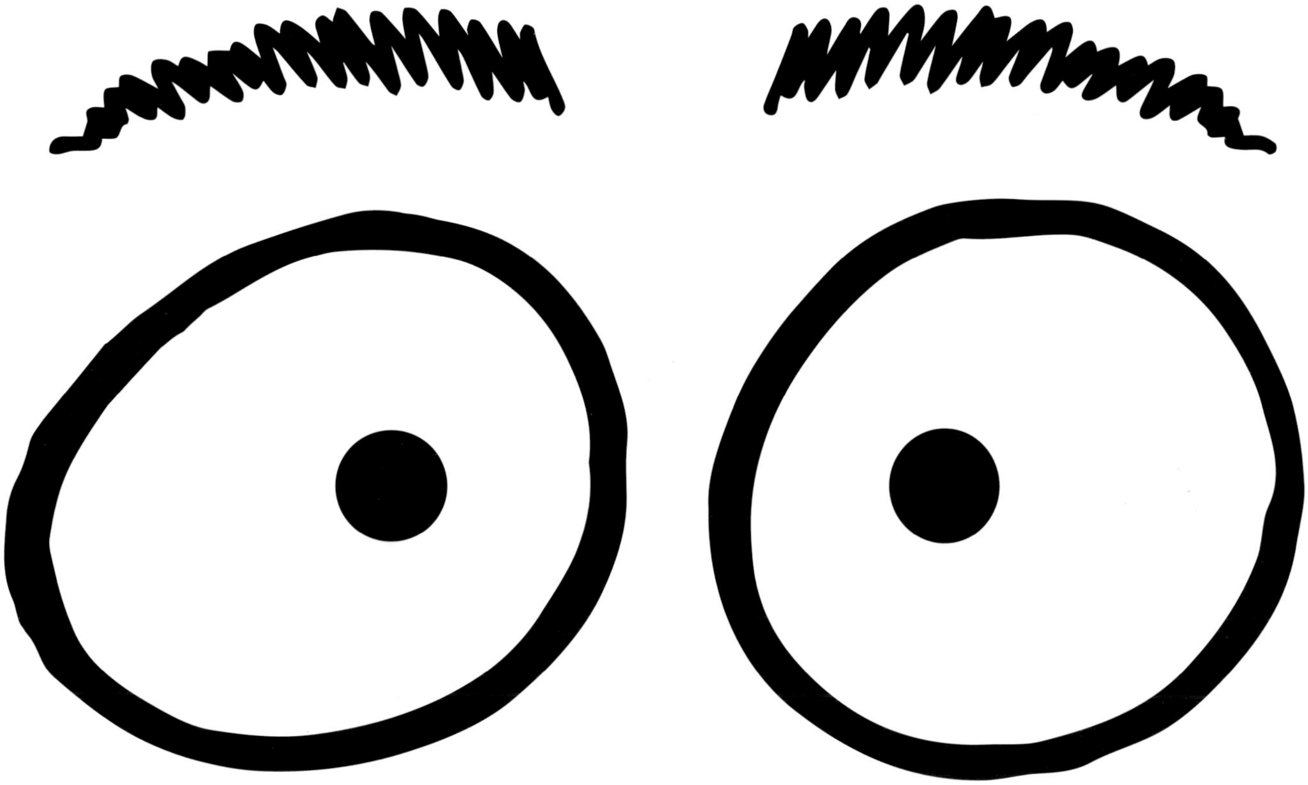

WHAT? You don't **BELIEVE** me?

I have the trophies and medals to prove it.

Wait here. I'll go get them!

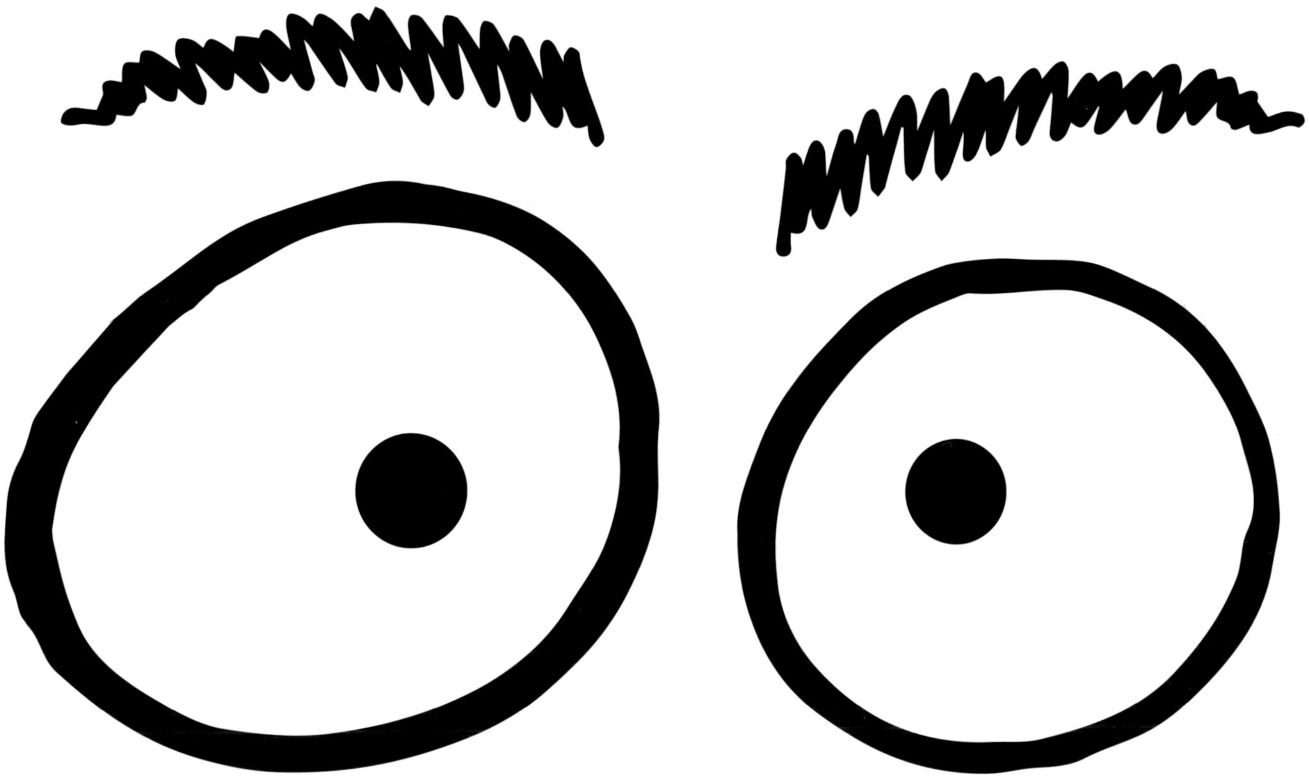

HEY! Wait a minute!

You're trying to make me lose.

I can't believe you tried to trick me.

That wasn't very nice of you.

You better be careful.

I've got my eyes on you.

Aren't you getting tired yet?

I bet your eyes are starting to burn.

Don't you have to go to the bathroom?

If I were you, I'd have to go to the bathroom.

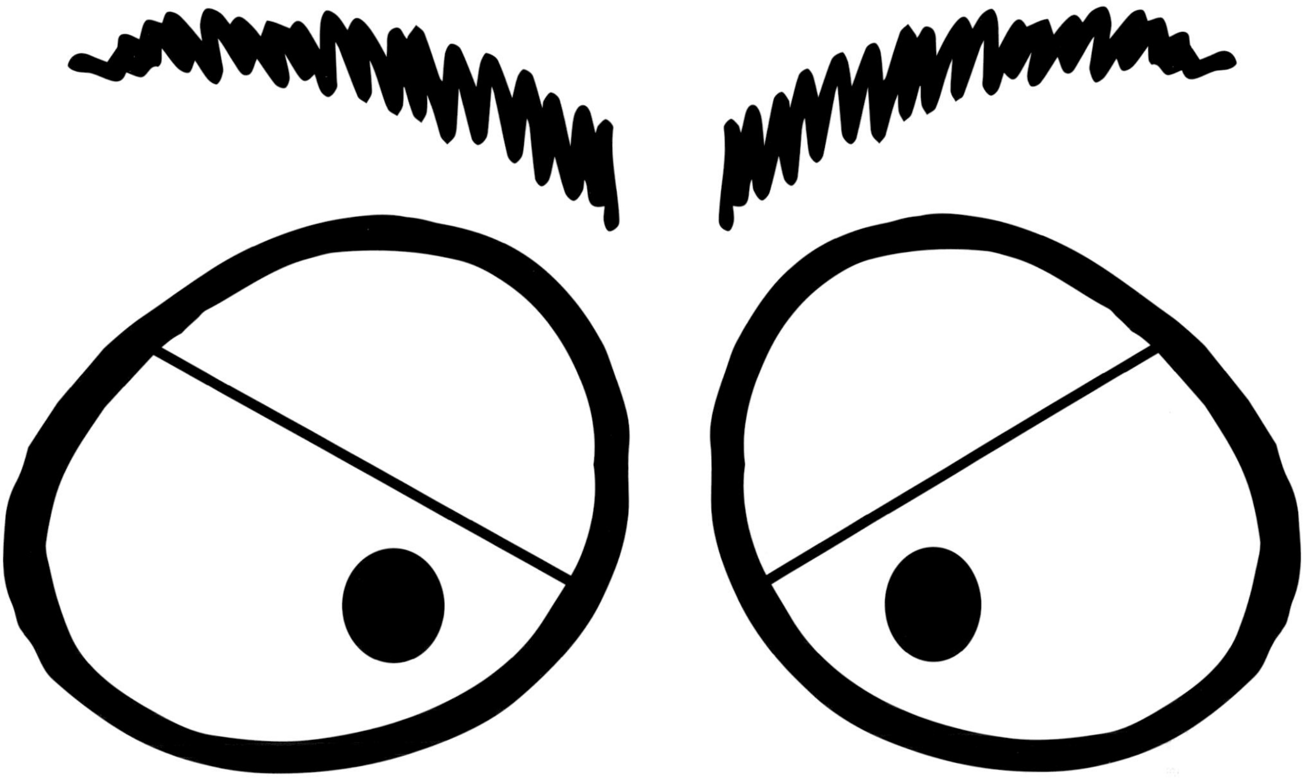

Uh-oh! I think **I** have to go to the bathroom.

And **I'M** getting tired,

and **MY** eyes are starting to burn!

I don't think . . .

I can keep . . .

them open . . .

any longer . . .

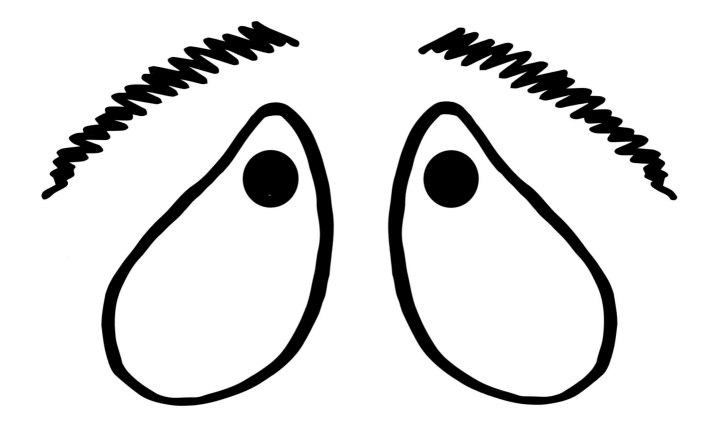

BLINK

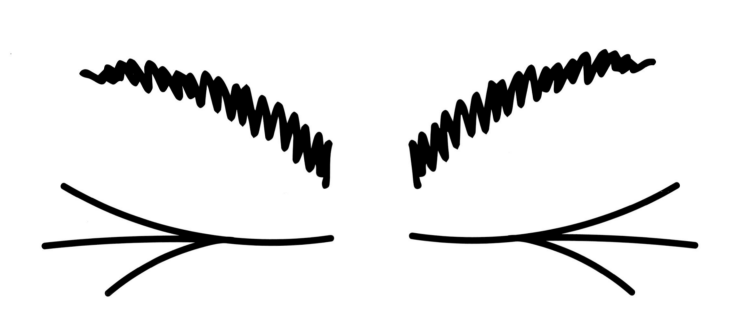

NOOOOO! I lost!

This is the worst day of my life!

I'll never play the staring contest game again . . .

ever.

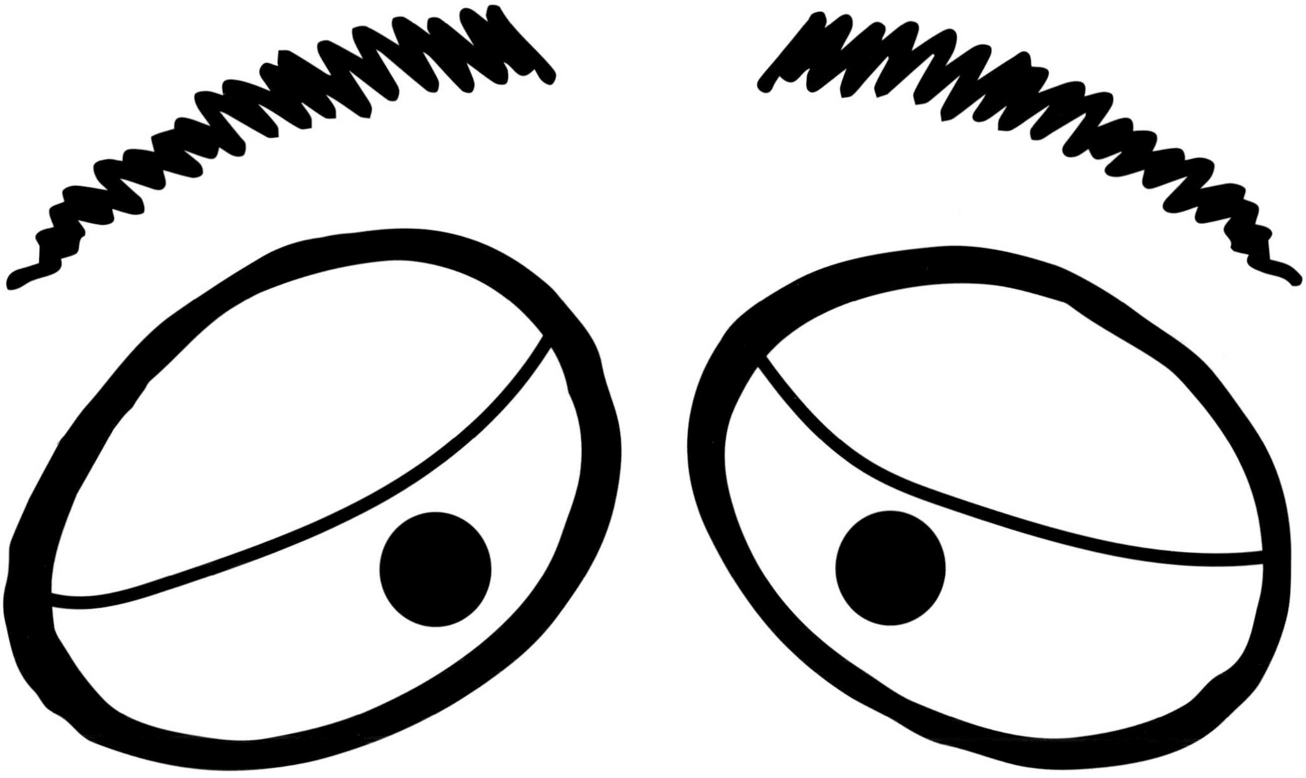

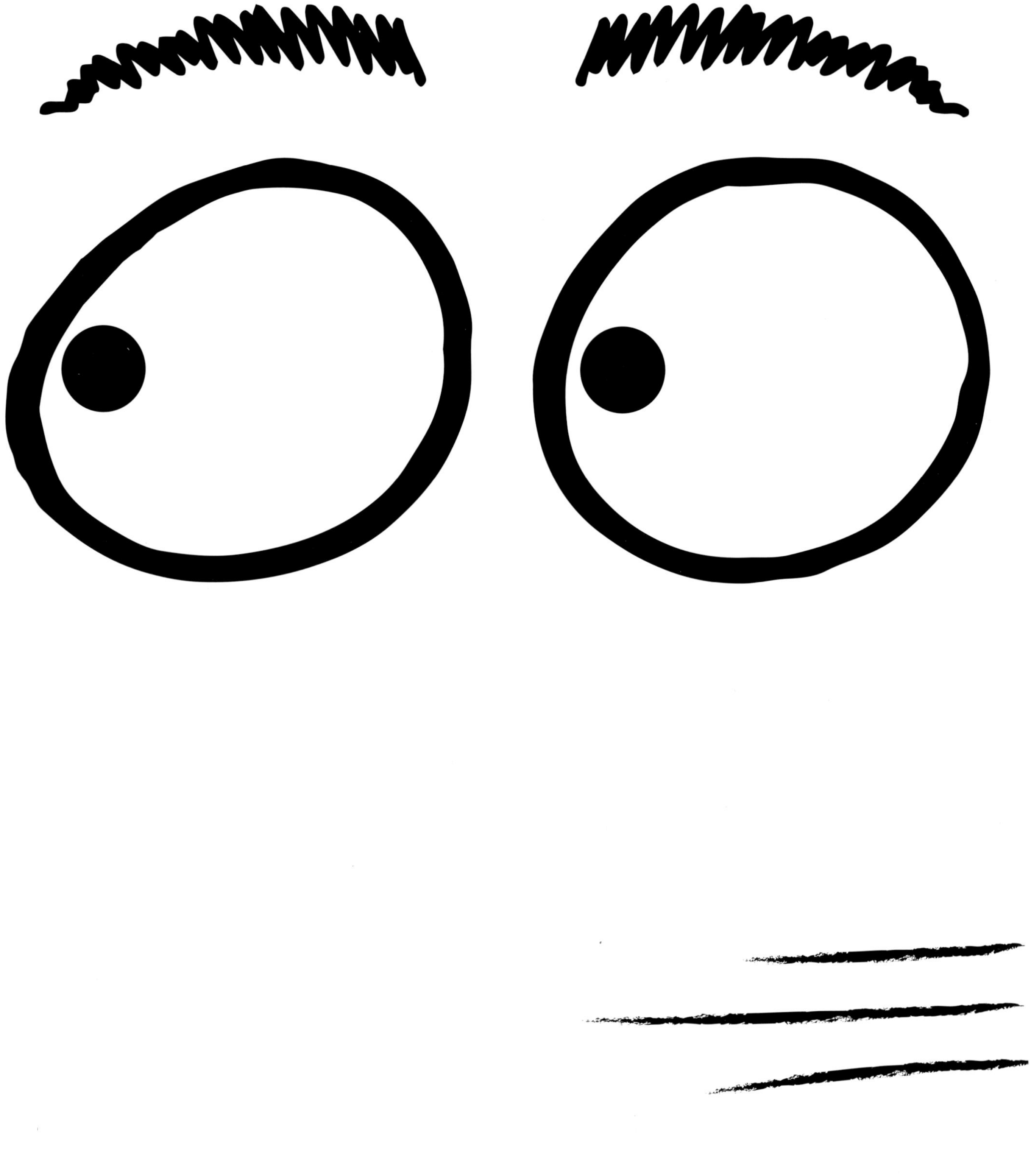

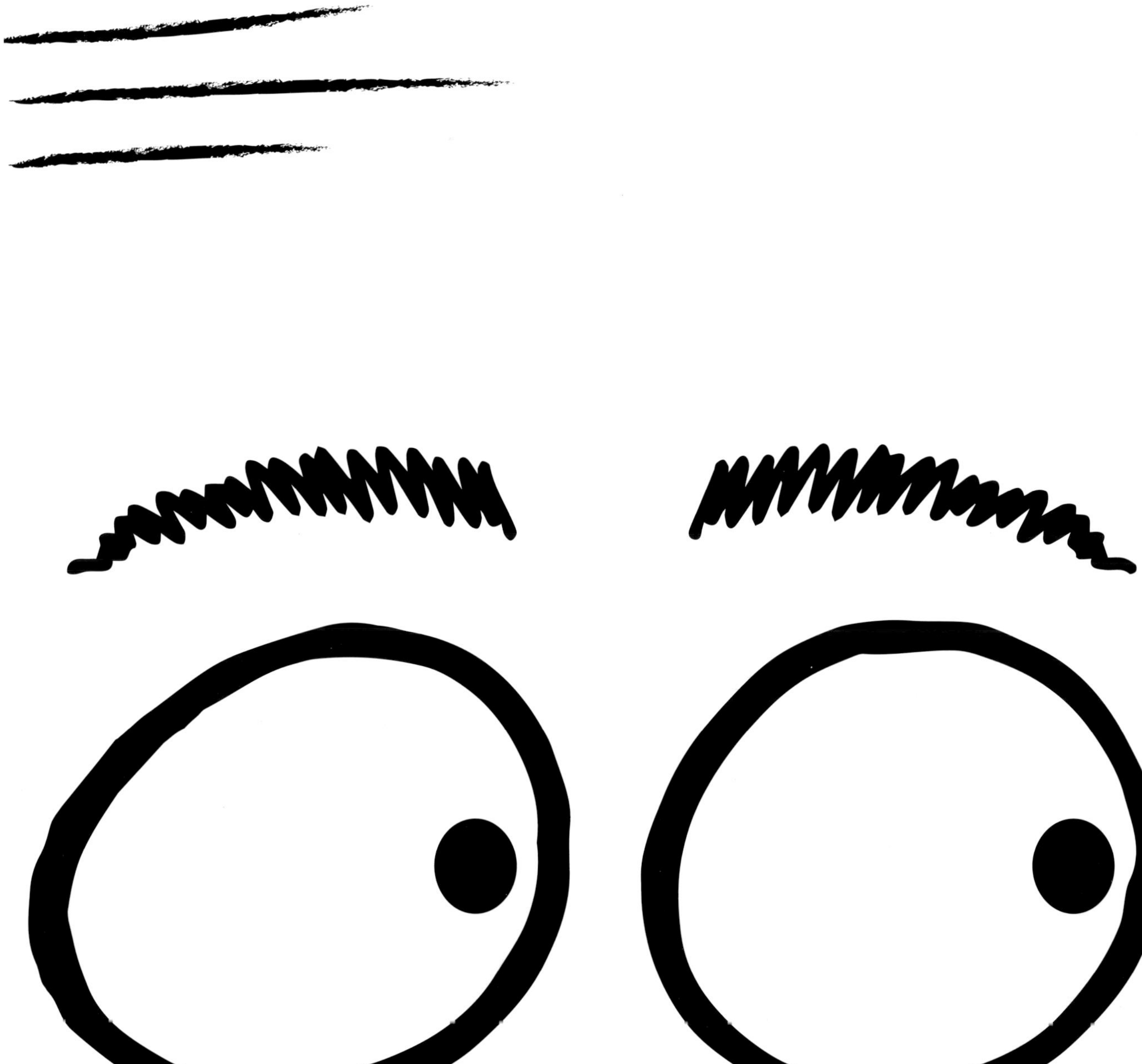

Best two out of three!

GO!

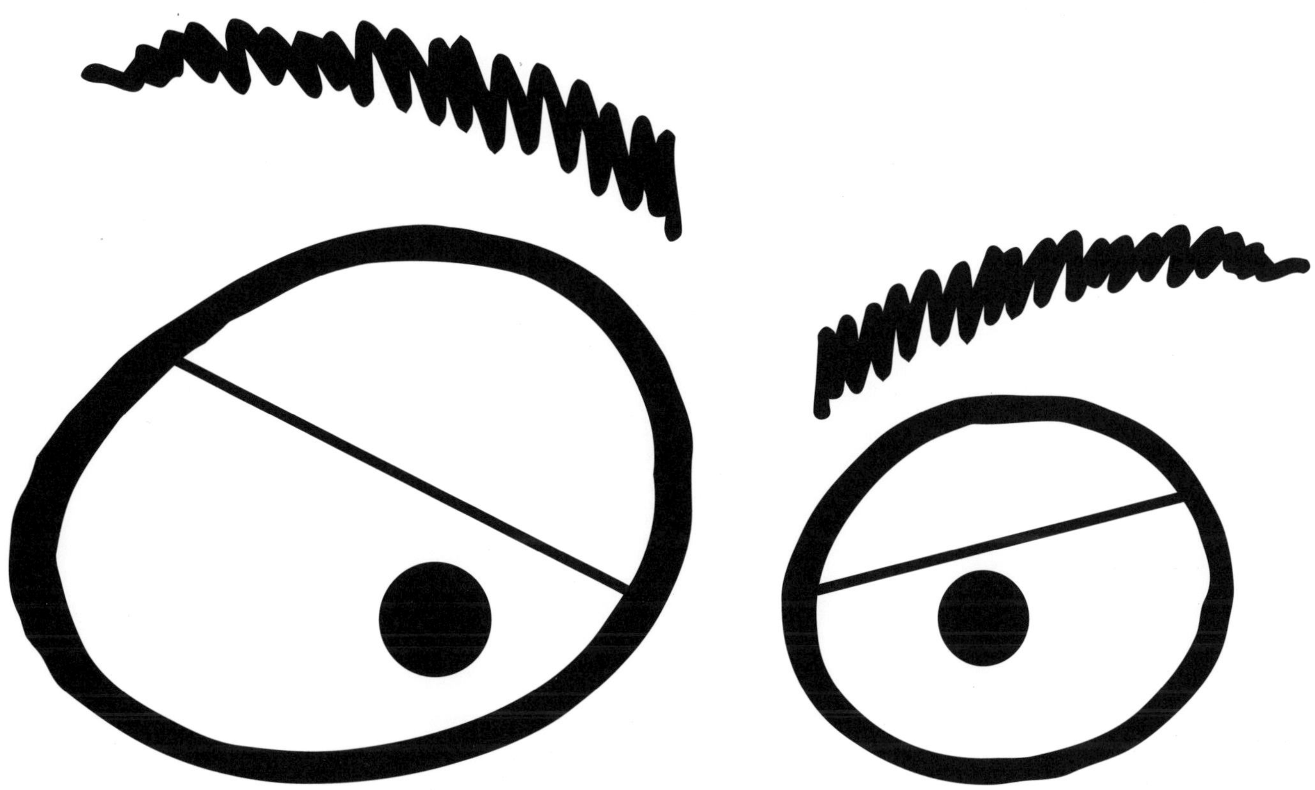